Crystalline And Bright

AMY LAURENS

OTHER WORKS

Find other works by the author at www.amylaurens.com

Crystalline And Bright

INKLET #75

AMY LAURENS

Inkprint PRESS

www.inkprintpress.com

Print ISBN: 978-1-922434-15-9
eBook ISBN: 9798201492847

www.inkprintpress.com

National Library of Australia Cataloguing-in-Publication Data
Laurens, Amy 1985 –
Crystalline And Bright
56 p.
ISBN: 978-1-922434-15-9
Inkprint Press, Canberra, Australia
1. Young Adult Fiction—Fantasy—Contemporary 2. Young Adult Fiction—Short Stories, Collections & Anthologies 3. Young Adult Fiction—Coming Of Age 4. Young Adult Fiction—Loners & Outcasts

First Print Edition: January 2022
Cover photo © Alex Perez via Unsplash
Cover design © Inkprint Press
Interior art © Amy Laurens

CRYSTALLINE AND BRIGHT

I STOOD, STARING DOWN INTO THE TEAL-blue river water, ignoring the chatter behind my back. The snow covered the ground around me, hiding bumps and ridges, soothing out sharp edges. To my right, the dark stone shadow of the bridge stood like a guardian, watchful, alert. Snow rimmed its edges; every so often some shifted in a sudden breeze and landed in the quiet river below with a gentle splash.

The willows on the far bank slept quietly under their snow blanket, their green sappy smell hidden by the cold, sharp scent of the snow.

Stop.

Start again.

It wasn't actually winter. It was early spring, with the grass green and new, the sound of a lawnmower buzzing in the distance and the scent of cut grass drifting on the wind. Moss covered the shadowed side of the old stone bridge, and willows stretched their fingers to the slow-moving, drowsy little river that bordered the grounds of the school.

A butterfly flittered past, white wings speckled with black like soot.

The world felt fresh, and green, and full of promise.

I was still ignoring the chattering behind me.

Stop.

Start again.

It's summer, and the air is swelteringly hot. Sweat drips down the back of my neck, pools under my arms, under my awkward breasts. The river in front of me is milky-blue, gentle, quiet, and I long to strip off my shirt and jeans and throw myself into the water.

It's not just the breathtakingly sharp cold of the icemelt I'm craving; it's the feeling of being *clean*.

The air stinks of a fish that Lander left out on the bank near the bridge, rotting to pieces in the high temperatures.

I'm still ignoring the chatter.

Stop.

Let's try once more.

It's autumn—of course—and the willows have turned yellow, their little leaves dropping into the milk-water, eddying slowly away from the shadow of the bridge.

Behind me, the emerald lawn of the old school buildings is ringed with gem-toned maples, butter-leafed poplars, silver-and-gold birches. Occasionally, the wind catches stray leaves and flings them into the pond.

I can still hear the voices behind me.

All of these pictures are true, and none of them are.

Not precisely, not uniquely; they're all composites, the merging and piecing together of hundreds of memories of similar experiences, of all the times I stood on the river bank and stared longingly into its depths, imagining myself a naiad with a secret home to return to, somewhere people loved me.

These images have to be composites, because for every time I was down at the river, I was focusing only on two things: ignoring the voices, and watching the water.

All the other details, the little bits of specificity that allow me to recall the place in so much explicit detail? I never noticed them at the time.

And so I have to piece them together, collage-fashion, or else I have nothing to say. Nothing to see.

Nothing except the water, milky-blue that occasionally, in the right light, at the right time of day, flashed teal and came alive.

I'd lived with the voices as long as I

could remember. Some of them were real, inasmuch as they belonged to real, live people whom other people could see, who grew and developed and changed with the passing of the seasons; some of them were *surreal*, inasmuch as they belonged to people I could see, but that none other could, and who did not change or grow with the passing of the seasons.

And some of the voices… Some of them I could never divine exactly what they were.

But all of them, real, surreal and unknown, had one thing in common: none of them liked me.

I could never figure out why. Oh, sure, I came to the school without the name and pedigree of any of the other students, a supposed-orphan with no memory of her life before double digits and no connections to speak of. I wasn't part of their circle, my excellent trust fund notwithstanding, and so the real people, the live people, couldn't accept me.

It shouldn't have been that way. It seemed to me that I hadn't done anything wrong, or untoward, hadn't neglected to do anything needed, hadn't slighted or snubbed any who hadn't already done so several times to me.

And yet, for all the years I was there at the school, its grand, lofty double-storey buildings made from pale stone like a castle, ivy creeping all about like Christmas lights, the lawn constantly emerald, the hedges consistently clipped... For all those composite years, no one ever liked me.

Well, a slight exaggeration: my teachers liked me well enough. I was a diligent student.

And the river liked me. I could tell that, because when I was close to the river, the other voices kept their distance—and the river had a voice of its own. And once or twice, I could have sworn it also had a face.

The first time I realised that one day I would escape was a crystalline autumn evening, golden sunlight dripping through the willows, the towering ashes that bordered the school along the river behind me dappling the grass as they caught and hoarded the light. The air was still, the river was slow, and the voices, for once, reduced to only those that I alone could hear; my fellow students were, for the most part, packing their rooms away in preparation for the autumn holidays, which began at 5pm that night.

Holidays were awkward.

No one came for me, but they could not hold the boarding house open for a mere one student, so I was shipped off to a hotel in the city, notionally under the guardianship of the principal—to whom I had been generically entrusted at the age of ten with an anonymous trust fund large enough to secure my private education and then some—but in actually, now that I was seventeen, fending for myself.

I didn't mind so much. The voices only I could hear were quieter in the city. Not distant, like they were when I was by the river, but quieter, their constant generic disapproval of my every action diminished by all the noise of the city itself—the traffic rushing and beeping, the whirr of a thousand machines, the crowded feel of electricity and waveforms clogging up the air. All of it seemed to drain the power of my invisible voices a little, enough that they grew dim with time.

You'd have thought, then, that I would have loved the city better than I did.

But for all that I spent every every holidays there, roaming streets that smelled of soot and exhaust, eating strawberry gelato and margarita pizza and watching endless hours of TV, the school was still my home. When I was away, I missed the green, green grass; I missed being surrounded by trees, as though living as a dryad in a forest; and I missed the river.

And so, on this quiet, final autumn afternoon, I had come down to the river to say farewell, to listen as the wrens danced through the willows, to dip my fingers into the coolness of the water and kiss it all goodbye.

The voices stood a way behind me, back on the green, green grass of the school grounds.

In front of me, the water threw the light in a way that made it seem bottomless.

And as I stretched down to meet the

water, the water stretched up to meet me.

My breath caught in my throat; for all the years I'd lived here, for all the years I'd loved the river, it had never loved me back. At least, not like this.

I swilled my fingers back and forth in the coldness, marvelling at the way the water lapped against gravity up my wrist, twining and trickling around my forearm.

The susurrus of voices behind me grew louder.

As they did, the spiralling web of water around my forearm grew stronger, gripping me with firm confidence and pulling me forward.

I had just enough time for my heart to squeeze in fear, for my breath to leave my mouth in a high-pitched squeak—and the river dragged me in, head first, the icy water shocking against the warmth of the afternoon.

I surfaced easily enough, long strands of my dark blonde hair caught in my mouth, matting over my eyes, and I trod water and scraped hair from my face and spat water that tasted slightly mineral away, and I was fine.

I scowled at the water around me. "What was that for?"

In the distance, I heard the voices laughing.

I could only be grateful, against the knot of embarrassment in my chest, that my classmates hadn't been here to witness this as well.

Around me, the water rippled, and I felt as though it laughed.

I splashed at it, trying to hold on to my irritation, my embarrassment—but in truth, the water cradled me like loving arms and I could no more be indignant at it than I could resent the sky.

I lay back, floating, sunlight sparkling on the drops of water that clung to my eyelashes. The water was cool, the sunlight was warm…

One day, not too far in the future, school would be over, and I'd be free of the anchored weight that kept me in this place.

And then a voice shouted from the shore. "Hey, Burly, your ride's here!"

I sighed, stroked for the shore, and emerged, sopping wet, by the bridge. I lifted the hem of my t-shirt, raised one foot and then the other—but the water streamed from me like I'd become the river itself, and I knew there was no point trying to dry. Deflated, I headed for the boarding house, steeling myself for the mockery I knew would greet me.

By the time I reached the foyer of the boarding house, however, a high-ceiling, dark room that smelled of must and age, there was no longer any reason for mockery: my clothes, my shoes, my hair? All perfectly dry.

I didn't understand—but I didn't have time to give it much thought. My chauffeur was here, and the matron of the boarding house clapped her big hands and shooed me upstairs to get my bags, and ten minutes later I was in the back of the sleek, black car, leaving the school grounds for a little over two weeks.

As the car pulled out onto the secluded country road that led back into town, I twisted, craning my neck for one last glimpse—not of the school, but of the river.

Surely I had imagined the river reaching up to grab me. Surely I had just overbalanced, inventing the loving caress of the river as a poor substitute for all the affection my living life lacked.

But I bit the inside of my lip and thought about the way the susurrus of voices had gotten louder, excited, as the river had reached up to me—and how even now, though I couldn't understand their words any more than I had ever been able to, the voices around me seemed electrified.

I pressed my fingers against the cool glass of the car window and daydreamed of milky-blue rivers and sparkling icemelt that winked and smiled in the sunlight.

The two weeks in the city felt endless. The weather had turned, the days short and chill, the leaves on the few extant trees turning crimson and scarlet and gold, and it made leaving my apartment difficult. Once I was out, wrapped in an ivory down jacket, my ice-blue scarf tucked about my throat, the cold wasn't so bad; it wasn't the fierce bite of winter yet, and the afternoon sun still held warmth—but it was an impediment, inertia that needed to be overcome to get out of the apartment every morning.

The holidays were a strange, timeless place in my life, without deadlines, without schedules—without any other human desire to intrude upon my own.

It had used to be lonely, but by the time of these holidays, with my eighteenth birthday tugging at my awareness—the Friday before I was due back at school—I'd acclimatised.

I hadn't always been alone. I felt certain of that. Every now and then, when I was exiting the shower or running the tap in the kitchen sink, I opened my mouth to call to someone over the noise... Only before I could speak, I remembered that I was alone, that there was no one here to call to.

In the first week of the holidays, though, just days after the river had pulled me in, I was washing my hair under a stream of hot water, steam clouding the bathroom air filled with the aroma of rose-geranium shampoo and aloe vera conditioner, and I felt it.

I stiffened, hands buried in the lathered suds of my long hair, water running hot down my back. "Hello?" It was the first time I'd actually managed to speak when that strange sensation—almost remembrance—of not being alone came over me.

"Adamaris?"

Adrenalin tugged in my chest. Adamaris? I didn't remember speaking that name before, and yet somehow the shape of it was familiar in my mouth.

The shower water ran cold, cold as the icemelt river.

I shrieked, leaping to the side of the shower, out of the flow of water—but the spray from the shower followed me, twining about my body, curving over my shoulders and down my spine, spiralling around my legs, my arms.

For the first time I could remember, the voices fell completely silent.

I stood, heart pounding, until the suds from my hair dripped into my eye. I hissed at the pain and winced, shoved my face under the water to wash it… And the water ran warm once more.

The rest of the holidays passed in a blur of cosy-chaired reading and bundled-up walks, stops at the cafe where I got my breakfast and lunch and quiet nights illuminated by the tungsten bulbs that reflected golden in the glass of the apartment windows.

My birthday passed largely unre-marked, aside from the letter from the bank declaring my trust fund to be, at last, my own, no intermediary required. I squeezed the bright blue card between my fingers and bit my lip to hide the grin.

I was so, so nearly free.

The terms of my trust fund had stipulated that I remain at the school until the age of eighteen, when the money could legally be mine, but there were no conditions attached as to what I had to do after that. Technically, I needn't even return to school for my final three terms... But it seemed silly to waste all the money that my generous, anonymous benefactor had invested into my education.

Still. I tapped the card against the tip of my nose, breathing in the sharp scent of the plastic, and grinned.

Nearly free. Nearly.

I didn't realise how nearly it was. When I woke up in the morning, my apartment was silent. For the first time I could remember, apart from that brief moment in the shower last week, the susurrus of disapproving voices was gone.

I tried out the familiar-yet-strange name on my tongue: "Adamaris?"

No one answered.

But the silence filled me with almost as much joy as any answer might have done. The voices were gone. I was free from their disapproval at last.

The day I returned to school, it was raining. Not a gentle, autumn rain that soaked the ground and raised the last crop of mushrooms before the cold of winter; no. This was a fierce gale, with raging winds driving the water almost horizontal, pushing me—and the car, and the spruce trees along the road—inevitably toward the school.

But despite the noise of the storm, for the first time, I was heading toward school in silence. The voices hadn't returned.

We pulled through the wrought-iron gates with leaves and twigs flappering madly at the car's roof and windscreen, and the chauffeur inched down a driveway barely visible through the rain and debris.

At the end of the drive, we stopped under the portico outside the boarding house foyer, and I leapt from the car, navy-blue woollen coat clutched tightly at my chin. The wind whipped my cheeks, my hair tugging to get free from the loose bun I'd tied it up in, and the chauffeur all but threw my bags on the doorstep before slamming the boot, re-entering the car, and high-tailing it as fast as he could safely go away from the school, and the storm.

I stood, staring after the red tail-lights that gleamed like eyes in the dim light, a strange sense of grief weighing down my chest. Wind snapped at me, spitting ice-cold rain in my face, the scent of wet stone and wet grass almost taking my breath away.

I had the strangest feeling that I would never see the chauffeur again.

Snorting at my whimsy, I shook my head, collected my bags, and headed for my room.

The storm blew itself out overnight, and the morning that dawned was crystalline and bright. A soft, pale sky gleamed like a fresh-water pearl and the smell of damp grass permeated even the must of the boarding house.

Before breakfast I was outside, crossing the debris-strewn lawn briskly, the hems of my jeans growing damp as I swished toward the river.

Through the silver birches that had been stripped of nearly all their leaves overnight, under the tall, tall ashes… Something tight in my chest eased as I glimpsed the milk-blue river. In the soft morning light, it seemed deeper teal than usual, and strange currents seemed to play in it. The river was usually slow and languid, but this morning, sticks and twigs eddied and twirled in the middle, flotsam and jetsam from the night's storm washed up along a high-water line a few feet above the level of the water.

I knelt beside it anyway, water soaking through the knees of my jeans in seconds.

I should have been freezing. The air

was chill and crisp, the world was damp and sleepy—and the river raced alongside me, rushing with a noise like the pouring rain, white foaming in lacy webs across its surface.

"You're in a hurry today," I murmured as I dipped my fingers into the icy flow.

It shocked me not at all when the river rippled up to meet me, bubbles and foam tracing ornamental lattices up my skin.

This time, I remembered to grab a breath before the water dragged me under. A good thing, too, because the current was even stronger than it had looked. It dragged me down, down, down, turning me, tumbling me like a rock.

I bashed against a boulder deep below the surface, crying out instinctively, grasping after the air as it left my lungs.

Tumble.

Tumble.

Which was way up?

I couldn't see the surface, couldn't hear anything but the roar of the water against my eardrums.

My lungs began to burn.

I pressed one hand over my mouth, pinching my nose. With the other, I stroked desperately, kicking out with all my strength, praying desperately that I'd find the surface.

Something brushed against me.

Too gentle for a rock, too large for a fish...

My chest contracted as I imagined what might be in the river. All those times I'd thought I'd seen an eye, a glimpse of a smile... The long, watery fingers that had reached up and pulled me in.

The creature bumped against me again, pressing against my side. My fingers caught at something that felt like hair. I clutched.

Faster than breathing, the thing I'd caught hold of raced through the water. The sudden increase in speed left my stomach somewhere at the bottom of the river—but we shattered through the surface into the sunlight and I gasped greedily at the air, scraping hair from my face, clinging at the creature that had saved me.

It nudged my cheek.

I squeezed water from my eyes, moved the last of my unruly hair—and stared into the huge, shining eye of a horse.

A horse, but it was teal and semi-transparent, made of water, white foam dripping down its neck in place of a mane, every bit as large and as real as a regular horse—only here, with me, in the stream.

It nudged at me again with its gentle nose.

My eyes were wide, my mouth open —and my fingers were entwined in its mane, and it had saved me.

The water-horse snorted, sending spray over my face. I flinched, then laughed. "Adamaris?" I asked, though it didn't feel quite right.

The horse clearly knew the name, however; it pivoted instantly, encouraging me vigorously to mount. So I did, and the horse sped down the river effortlessly like a dolphin, milky-blue and white and crystal bright. The fresh, mineral tang of the water coated my lips and cold air buffeted my cheeks and the tip of my nose.

I'd never been above the bridge before—at least, not that I could remember—but there was nothing to do now but cling tightly to a horse made of water and foam and laugh as the spray from our passing glittered in the sunlight now cresting over the treetops.

High up in the mountains, the river dwindled to a stream, deep and purposeful—and cold as it passed into a crevice in the rocks, hidden from the sun. Dark rock walls narrowed to either side until I could have brushed my fingers against them with out-stretched arms, had we not been trav-elling so fast I feared I'd injure myself if I tried.

Abruptly, my darling teal water-horse reared. It seemed that surely I should fall off—but I stayed as securely mounted as if the horse had merely drawn to a gradual halt.

My chest lightened. I breathed deeply of cold air that smelled of mineral water and mountain rock and moss.

The horse replanted its feet, tossing its head at a narrow gap in the rocks ahead, from whence this mountain river was born.

"Am I supposed to go in there?" I said, not sure what sort of answer I could expect.

But the horse tossed its head clearly enough, so I slipped from its back, heart pitter-pattering in my chest, and climbed the small, smooth boulders to the gap. Green algae slicked the rocks, slimy under my hands, but I didn't slip, and I didn't fall. The water splashing over my arms, leaping at my legs, was like ice—but I didn't feel the cold.

Instead, my heart pounded faster with strange anticipation. I scrambled through the gap, rough stone pressed on either side—and inside, in the darkness, over the rushing noise of the stream that covered me to mid-thigh, the voices returned.

Disappointment stabbed me. My jaw twitched. I hadn't missed the voices, or their constant disapproval of my life.

But... I tilted my head.

Somehow, even through the noise of the stream, the voices seemed a little clearer now, as though if only the water would quiet, I might actually understand them.

Hesitant, water dripping from my hair, my eyebrows, my nose, I stepped forward.

Deep in the depths of the cave, blue light flared.

My breath caught in my chest; I forgot for a moment how to move.

But the stream that still flowed around me lapped gently, reaching up to twine around my hips and waist, a soft and gentle encouragement filled with that same sense of liking I'd always felt from it.

And so, after a deep inhale of mineral-rich air, I waded toward the light.

The rushing of the stream and the susurrus of voices drowned out my thoughts, like moving through a dream, one swishing, swirling, laboured step after another. I couldn't tell if it was a handful of minutes or an arm-load, but soon the light grew close.

It wasn't a light.

Well, it was, but there was more than one—and they weren't simply lights. They were people.

They were the voices.

And as I drew close, at last I could understand them.

"Ridiculous decision, sending her out like that."

"What did they think was going to happen if something went wrong?"

"Can't believe they left her with nothing but us for protection."

"They didn't *think*."

"Constantly in danger, no idea who she is…"

"…how can she even decide?"

I couldn't stand. My heart was pounding so hard it might burst out of my chest, and I couldn't stand up another moment.

I sank to the rocks at the side of the stream, the narrow cave lit only by the blue glow of these beings that glimmered and glinted off the tealy-blue water, my hand gripping tightly against the wall.

It sounded… I swallowed, blinked, shook my head.

These were the same voices that had followed me as long as I could remember. I even recognised some of the beings as the people that had haunted my vision, the ones I'd quickly learned that others couldn't see, the ones who didn't grow or change or develop.

I'd recognise their tone of disapproval anywhere. But if what I was hearing was true… it wasn't me they disapproved of.

"Adamaris?" I said, quiet, full of longing, my chest a gaping hole of amnesia.

The beings quelled at once and stared at me.

"She remembers," one murmured, the elderly woman with the long, long hair and eyes as sharp as flint.

As one, they parted.

I gasped.

The world reeled.

My fingers tightened against the rocks, seeking something stable, something steadying.

Because a woman was approaching from between the beings in blue light crystalline and bright, a real woman, not something ephemeral like the blue-glowing voices, and she was tall, and the hair that spilled from her brow in soft and gentle waves to her waist was a darkish blonde, like mine, until it melted into the water of the stream, and the ice-blue eyes that smiled at me above a gently curving mouth were my eyes that stared back at me from the mirror, and although I couldn't remember anything, I couldn't imagine how I could ever forget her.

"Adamaris?" I said, and my voice trembled in the dark over the sound of the rushing stream. "Mum?"

The woman whose body ceased at the level of the water melted, collapsing toward me, enfolding me in her arms and hugging me tight against her chest. "Oh, Amberly. Oh, my darling Amberly. You made it." She kissed my hair, pushed me out to arm's length to look me over in the dim blue light, held me to her again. "Oh Amberly," she said against my wet hair. "You made it."

I wasn't cold, I realised, not because because my mother's arms were wrapped around me for the first time in eight years. And not because I simply wasn't noticing the water.

I wasn't cold because my body *was* the water.

I was water, I was flesh, I was my mother's daughter—and after a long, long absence, I was home.

THE MAKING OF *CRYSTALLINE AND BRIGHT*

I think that maybe this is one of my favourite of all the short stories I've written in my life so far. That seems like a big claim, but... I think it's accurate?

Weirdly, this story was inspired by a small part of the film *Frozen 2*, the part where Elsa tames the hostile northern oceans, and an ice horse appears to speed her on her way.

I love horses; I love the ocean (even though I'm always nervous when swimming in it). So after viewing the film for the first time, in an open-air pop-up cinema on the shores of the lake as the summer sun set in a clear blue sky, I knew I wanted to write something that captured that moment for me.

I sat down to write the opening… and it didn't feel right.

But instead of deleting it, I wrote the next line:

Stop. Start again.

I did start again… And again… And then I realised: those stoppings, and restartings? That wasn't the story going wrong. That *was* the story.

I wonder how often in life we might feel like we're going down the wrong path, longing for a sense of progress and direction… only to discover much later on that the path we were on was the right one after all.

P.S. Fun facts, I had no idea that Amberly was the name of the main character in the TV adaptation *The Shannara Chronicles* when I picked it for this story. I just thought it sounded like it matched with Adamaris :D

Read more by Amy Laurens!

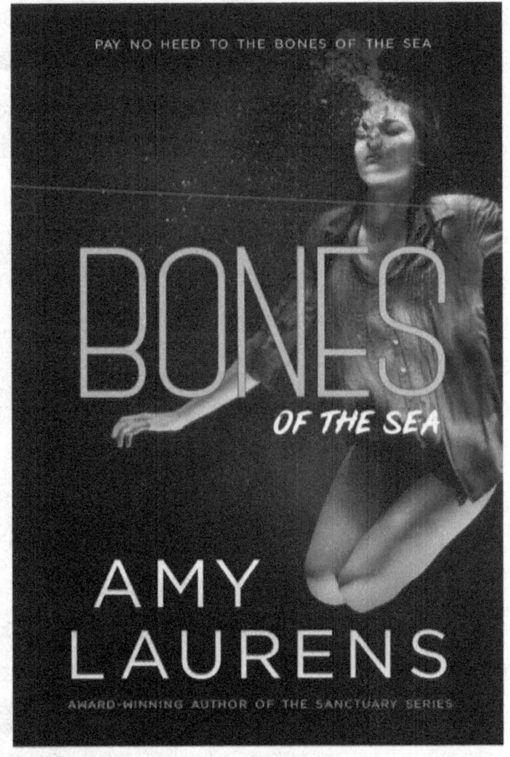

BONES OF THE SEA

THE MAN—WHOSE NAME IS IRRELEVANT, for he shall soon be dead—wandered down the beach where sand whiter than any he'd seen before swashed between a short, head-high cliff to his left, and the frothing waves of the ocean to his right. Salt filled the air, but below that, something else lingered, and he couldn't quite place his... nose... on what it was.

Of course, the locals were horrified that he was here at all. But he was a Man Of Learning, and was not accustomed to heeding the warnings of people obviously less learned than himself, especially when they spoke tales of a beach that left no trespasser alive.

He'd scoffed. Ridiculous, their legends of a beach where to set one toe on the sand was to seal your own death sentence before the rising of the next full moon.

He was far more interested in ana-
lysing the sand, quite literally whiter
than any he'd seen before, and thus far
resistant to his attempts to decode it.
He'd thought a pure variety of quartz
before he'd arrived, but upon reaching
the beach, pulling into the little de-
serted cul-de-sac dead end festooned
with warning signs ('Cursed Beach, Do
Not Enter'; 'Beware The Bones Of The
Sea'), he'd switched his engine off,
opened the car door to the sound of
waves and wind through the saltbush,
and he'd seen the sharp drop-off down
to the sand and had changed his mind
to chalk, or maybe gypsum.

But there'd been no tiny fossils his
portable microscope could detect, and
the sand, whatever it was made from,
had failed to fizz under the application
of a drop of acid from his little glass
vial, so that struck gypsum and chalk
from the list of options.

Now, after several hours on the

beach to no avail as the hot evening sun seared his hands and the light glinting off both ocean and white sand blinded him, he'd had enough. He'd run out of fresh water, ideas, and patience all, and was presently hiking back around the cove to his car that glinted silver and tantalising at the far end of the beach, a haven of cool air and fresh water.

Stay. Stay a little while longer.

The salt clung to his skin, filming his lips, the inside of his nose, the back of his throat. Somehow, the ocean smelled sharper here, more concentrated. Briefly, he wondered if that was the source of the townsfolk's rumours; but a higher salt concentration ought to have meant people floated better, drowned less. No. There must simply be a convergence of factors that meant the currents here were particularly treacherous, and indeed, casting his gaze out to the distant horizon, examining the interplay of wave and off-white foam, the cove did seem to be quite swirly, with a few smooth tracts he thought were probably rips.

As ever, folklore had a logical series of explanations behind it.

Just a little longer.

His leather sandal caught on something in the sand.

He stumbled.

Ow. That hurt.

Whatever it was, it had poked through the holes in his footwear to stab at his toes.

Glaring, impatient, our nameless victim kicked away some of the strange, defiant white sand—and inhaled sharply.

Once the initial burst of adrenalin subsided—something a surprise human skull will inevitably inspire, regardless of one's general composure—it seemed obvious.

Of course. The one thing he hadn't tested for was bone.

So focused on unlocking the mystery of the sand's composition was he that his initial reaction was deep, gleeful satisfaction.

Dawning understanding, however, made him lift his feet, hesitantly at first, shaking the white sand—bone—sand, think of it as sand, it's safer that way—but it's bone, really it's bone, it's all bone, every single grain of it, pure white, sun-bleached bone, spat up from the guts of the ocean the way a predatory owl spits out the bones of its prey—and then his feet were dancing, just like his stomach, as he leapt for the cliff and tried to haul himself up and off the beach because God, oh God, he was standing on bones and only bones, and the skull he'd uncovered had been human, and there, just down the beach, that rock wasn't a rock, it was another skull, and oh

God, how many people had died here?

He realised the sobbing was his, rasps of panic as he scrabbled at the embankment that should have been easier to climb than it was, his fingers digging at the rock, skin tearing, sandals scraping for purchase…

Stay.

His back was to the ocean when the freak wave rose, a local tsunami of salt and hunger.

It smashed into him.

As it dragged him out to sea, all he felt was cold, so bitter it froze his bones right in his body.

An hour later, as the sun spilled red-orange lifeblood out over the ocean, the ocean spat a skull, bleached-white and grinning, back up onto the beach. A moment later, as the full moon crested over the craggy headland behind, a sternum—*most* of its ribs still attached—joined the skull, followed a moment later by a single scapula.

And as the moon rose and the ocean swallowed the sun, a whisper began that sounded like the wind… until you realised there was nothing but salt-bush for the wind to disturb, and the whispers sounded strangely like a voice, hungry, crooning, and singing.

Feed me.

Feeed mee.

Feeeed meeeeee….

Keep reading! Head to
<u>www.inkprintpress.com/ amylaurens/bonesofthesea/</u>
to buy your copy now!

AMY LAURENS is an Australian author of fantasy fiction for all ages. Honestly, if she could have a water horse like this one, she could probably quit striving for anything else and call her life won.

Amy has also written the award-winning portal-fantasy *Sanctuary* series about Edge, a 13-year-old girl forced to move to a small country town because of witness protection (the first book is *Where Shadows Rise*), the humorous fantasy *Kaditeos* series, following newly graduated Evil Overlord Mercury as she attempts to acquire a castle, the young adult series *Storm Foxes*, about love and magic and family in small town Australia, and a whole host of non-fiction.

Find her at www.AmyLaurens.com.

INKLET #079
Shadows
NEVER LIE
AMY LAURENS

INKLET #080
Here She Lies
LIANA BROOKS

INKLET #081
Perfect
Destruction
An Age Of Unicorns Story
AMY LAURENS

INKLET #082
What Blood
Can Do
AMY LAURENS

INKLET #083
Dancer, Dreamer
Seer
LIANA BROOKS

INKLET #084
As Time
Whirls Slowly
Past
AMY LAURENS

INKLET #085
Far More
Satisfying
Than Hell
AMY LAURENS

INKLET #086
Just
Another Day
In Hell
LIANA BROOKS

INKLET #087
Moon AND
Morning
AMY LAURENS

Some
Impropriety
Expected
AMY LAURENS

NEON SNOW
LIANA BROOKS

Reincarnation
LIANA BROOKS

More Than
Mushrooms
AMY LAURENS

DOUBLE ISSUE
How To Make A Star
& The World Ended
LIANA BROOKS

CAUGHT
IN THE ACT
AMY LAURENS

ANUBIS
Has Sent You
Six Souls
LIANA BROOKS

PRAYER TO A
GODDESS
LIANA BROOKS

Love In The
Time Of Corona
AMY LAURENS